FESTIVAL!

Ramadan and Eid ul-Fitr

Olivia Bennett

Contents

The Commonwealth Institute was opened in 1962 as the United Kingdom centre for the understanding of the countries and values of the Commonwealth, through education, exhibitions and the arts.

Education programmes have been offered to well over 100 000 children at the Institute each year and many more are reached through extramural programmes and publications.

In pursuing its objectives, the Institute has been responsible for a number of new initiatives, none of which has been more rewarding than its Festivals programmes for schools, which enable many hundreds of children to participate in the celebration of some of the Commonwealth's most significant cultural events. We feel strongly that this opportunity should be offered more widely to teachers and children and are delighted to be able to share in this venture with Macmillan. We trust that this publication will be of assistance to those wanting to know more about Britain's increasingly multicultural society and the wider world in which we live.

James Porter

Director of the Commonwealth Institute

M Macmillan Education

Watching for the moon

As the sun sets at the end of another long, hot day in Brunei, the Omar Ali Saifuddin mosque turns black against the red sky. It is the city's main building of worship for Muslims.

But this evening Brunei doesn't settle down for the night as quickly or as quietly as usual. For tomorrow is a special day for Muslims. The month of Ramadan is nearly over and tomorrow is the first day of the festival of Eid ul-Fitr. All over the world, Muslims are looking forward to several days of festivities which celebrate the end of a month of daytime fasting.

Preparations for celebrations

In their homes people are giving the final touches to new clothes. Sweets and other foods are being prepared. Families decorate their homes with colourful Eid cards which friends and relatives have sent. Shops and markets are crowded with people buying

▲ Many Muslim women paint delicate patterns and flowers in henna on their hands before the Eid celebrations at the end of Ramadan.

◀ The Omar Ali Saifuddin mosque, Brunei, at sunset. Brunei is a small country in South-East Asia. Over half the population are Muslim.

▲ Muslims send each other greeting cards and offer visiting friends and relatives delicious sweets and fruits during Eid ul-Fitr.

presents, food and coloured bangles to match their new outfits. The mosques are full of people at prayer. The streets are full of people greeting each other and watching the darkening sky for the silver arc of the new moon.

The Islamic year is divided into twelve months which follow the cycles of the moon. So this new moon will mark the end of Ramadan and the start of the next month — and the celebrations of Eid ul-Fitr. There is a feeling of excitement and happiness throughout the city.

And all over the world, Muslims are feeling the same excitement and anticipation. In some northern countries, such as Britain, the sky is sometimes too cloudy to see the new moon. So Muslim communities there keep in touch with Muslims in neighbouring countries, so that they know exactly when the moon is first sighted.

The celebrations begin

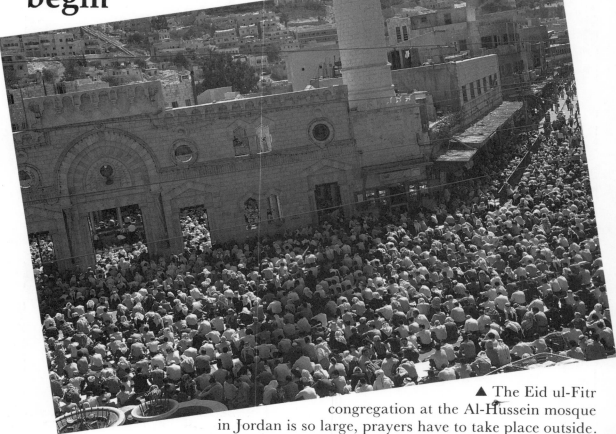

▲ The Eid ul-Fitr congregation at the Al-Hussein mosque in Jordan is so large, prayers have to take place outside.

The first day of Eid ul-Fitr begins with an early meal. Then families go to the mosque to give thanks to God and rejoice in having successfully gone without food and drink all day, every day, for a month. Sometimes there are so many people that these congregational prayers take place outside the mosque, in a large open space. Thousands of Muslims join together in thanksgiving and worship on this morning in Brunei, knowing that all over the world millions of other Muslims are doing the same. Wherever they are, not only will they be repeating the same prayers and feeling the same happiness, they will be turned towards the same holy spot in Saudi Arabia. Whether in Bangladesh or Britain, Turkey or Tunisia, Muslims always turn in the direction of their holy city of Makkah when they pray. And we too shall turn in that direction now, for it is there that the story of the religion of Islam begins.

Arabia at the time of Muhammad's birth.

Spain

Mediterranean

Persia

North Africa

Egypt

· Madina

· Makkah

Arabia

India

Arabian Sea

The religion of Islam

Muslims believe in one God. The Arabic name for God is Allah and the Arabic word 'Islam' means 'submission to the will of God'. A Muslim is one who 'submits to' or obeys God. The prophet, or messenger, of Allah was Muhammad. It was through him that God's teachings were revealed to the world. These were eventually written down in the Qur'an, which is the holy book of Islam.

Muslims believe that the words of the Qur'an are God's exact words as he gave them to Muhammad. Muhammad didn't rewrite or alter these words. He memorised and later dictated them to writers exactly as he had heard them, word for word. Ramadan is special because it was during this month that Muhammad began to receive God's messages, near the city of Makkah, over 14 centuries ago.

The story of Muhammad

The minaret of the Prophet's mosque, ▶ Madina, where Muhammad is buried. It was in this city that Muhammad established the first Muslim community.

The words Muhammad received from ▶▶ God are contained in the Qur'an, the holy book of Islam.

◀ Makkah, Saudi Arabia. The square black shrine, the Ka'aba, is believed to have been used in Old Testament times by Abraham. In Muhammad's time it was full of the idols which people worshipped. Muhammad turned it back into a 'house of God'. It remains Islam's most sacred place. Muslims all over the world turn in its direction to pray, and hope to visit it once in their lifetime.

Muhammad was born in Makkah in 570. In Muhammad's time the country was called Arabia. It was a wild and lawless place. Fierce tribes roamed the desert, fighting each other and attacking merchants. Quarrels between tribes and families were vicious and sometimes lasted years. People worshipped many different idols and believed in magic and evil spirits.

Muhammad's parents died when he was very small and he was brought up by relatives. When he was young he worked as a shepherd. He grew up to be a particularly kind and wise man and soon started work as a merchant. He trekked across the desert with long camel caravans, carrying silks and spices from the East to trade in the Mediterranean. In a world where honesty was rare, Muhammad became known as someone people could trust. A wealthy widow called Khadija took him on as manager of her trading business. She grew to love his honesty, wisdom and kindness and later they married.

Muhammad became a wealthy and respected member of the city of Makkah. But he was not really

content. The world he saw around him was a violent and often cruel place. He felt there must be more meaning to life than this. He used to go away quietly by himself and think deeply about the mysteries and problems of life.

A message from God

One of his favourite places to go at these times was a cave in Mount Hira, outside the city. One day when he was thinking quietly in this cave, an angel came to him. 'Recite' said the angel, whom Muslims believe was Gabriel. Muhammad was terrified. The Angel Gabriel repeated the command and Muhammad realised the words were being given to him. So he recited the message from God that Gabriel had brought him, until he knew it by heart.

These visits from Gabriel continued for many years. At first, Muhammad had been very frightened and over-awed by what had happened. He told Khadija, who was a great support to him. Gradually Muhammad came to believe that God really had chosen him to be His messenger to the world.

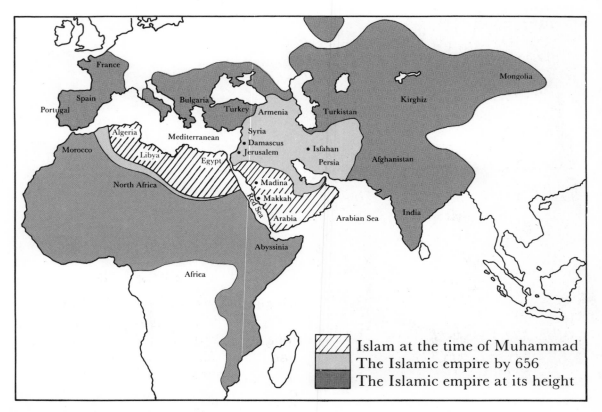

Islam at the time of Muhammad
The Islamic empire by 656
The Islamic empire at its height

▲ The spread of the Islamic empire.

Telling the world

Muhammad thought deeply about God's words and what they meant. It was three years before he felt ready to tell others of God's message. Then he began to preach in the streets of Makkah and tell people how God wanted them to live and worship. He asked them to give up their violent quarrels and selfish behaviour. He taught that God wished them to be merciful and kind. He told them that they should help others less fortunate than themselves.

Some people just laughed at him. Some took no notice. Others got very angry. A few did believe he was God's prophet, and they became the first Muslims. But their numbers grew very slowly. Sometimes they were attacked. Eventually they were forced out of Makkah and fled to a city now known as Madina.

Slowly, over many years, Muhammad's message reached the hearts of more and more people. Eventually all the tribes of Arabia became Muslims. Muhammad returned to Makkah which became the centre of the Islamic empire.

8

◀ Muslims treat their holy book, the Qur'an, with the utmost respect. They often decorate copies into magnificent works of art, to show the importance and beauty of the words they contain.

The last of the prophets

Muslim rulers allowed the Jews and Christians to practise their own religions. Muslims believe that God had also spoken to the world through Jewish and Christian prophets such as Moses, Abraham, David and Jesus. Muhammad himself had proudly told people how he, like David and Moses, had been a shepherd boy. It is hard to control a flock of sheep or goats who don't know the difference between right and wrong. People said that the patience and understanding a shepherd needs to lead his flock was good training for these prophets, who later had to lead people to God.

Islam teaches that Muhammad was the last and final prophet and the only one to record God's words exactly. God's earlier messages were sometimes ignored, or not fully obeyed. Only the Qur'an, Muslims believe, contains God's own, unchanged words.

Spreading the message

Muhammad had memorised the words of God exactly as they had been revealed to him. When he taught others, they also learnt them by heart. As time went by, Muhammad dictated God's messages to followers who wrote them down. It was not until after his death that these writings were gathered together into one book, the Qur'an.

Exact copies of the first book were made and placed in the main cities of the Islamic empire. Within a hundred years this stretched as far as Jerusalem, Babylon, Damascus and Isfahan.

Mosques and scriptures

The Star mosque, Dhaka, Bangladesh. ▶
Some Muslims are washing before saying their prayers. In the decorated prayer hall is the mihrab, which shows the direction of Makkah and the Ka'aba.

Kano mosque, northern Nigeria. ▶▶
There are many million Muslims in sub-Saharan Africa. Most of them are in West Africa, especially in northern Nigeria.

◀ The Omar Ali Saifuddin mosque, Brunei. Look closely, and you'll see the dome covering the prayer hall, the tall towers called minarets, and an open courtyard with shady cloisters and cool water.

The Qur'an was first written down in Arabic, the language of Arabia. Muslims felt it should be written in a way that showed the importance and beauty of its message. They developed the Arabic script into some of the most beautiful lettering in the world. The pages of the Qur'an are often like works of art, decorated by the shapes of the letters themselves, and with flowers and patterns. But they never show drawings of people or living creatures as illustrations. Muslims believe it would be wrong to copy God's own work by drawing pictures of the living things which He created.

The mosques on these pages are decorated in the same way, with letters, flowers, patterns and shapes of many colours. The beauty of the buildings themselves, with their graceful arches and domes, is another way in which Muslims have used their artistic skill to praise God.

There are many different styles of mosque. As Islam spread through Europe, Asia and Africa, different countries developed their own special designs. Most mosques, however, have certain things in common. A dome covering the prayer hall is one. A tall spire, called a **minaret**, is another.

A man called a **muezzin** calls people to prayer five times a day from the minaret. The tall tower helps his voice to carry a long way. Today, loudspeakers may also help. Usually there is a courtyard with a pool or fountain, or a room with taps for washing before prayer.

Inside the mosque, a niche in one wall indicates the direction of Makkah. This is the **mihrab**. There may also be a raised platform from where the prayer leader can give talks. This is the **minbar**. Near it you may find a low reading stand for the Qur'an. The floor of the prayer hall is usually covered with mats or carpets. Mosques are buildings of study as well as worship. There may be rooms where local people, especially children, can meet and learn the teachings of the Qur'an.

Muslims have built some of the most beautiful buildings of worship in the world. The feeling of space and the bright colours and patterns of the mosques impressed many European designers and architects. Some have tried to use the same ideas in their own work.

The Five Pillars of Islam

▼ The five daily prayers are said to a set of movements. Two of these are shown here. After touching the floor with the nose and forehead between the palms of the hands, Muslims sit upright with their hands on their thighs. They then repeat the two movements. These boys are kneeling on a prayer mat.

Although there are many different styles of mosque, they all follow a similar pattern. This is because their design expresses certain ideas about God and worship which are important to Muslims everywhere. For example, the importance of washing before prayers and of facing the direction of Makkah for prayer, means that a fountain, pond or some taps, and a mihrab will be found in almost all mosques.

Daily prayer is one of the five main duties of Islam, which all Muslims try to keep. The Five Pillars of Islam are the basis on which their faith is built, in the same way that the pillars of a building are strong and provide its support.

The First Pillar of Islam is to say with complete faith that 'There is no God but Allah and Muhammad is his prophet.' The Second Pillar is to perform the five daily prayers. The times of prayer are first thing in the morning (**fajr**), around midday (**zuhr**), in the middle of the afternoon (**'asr**), at sunset (**maghrib**), and at night (**'isha**).

The timing of the five daily prayers.

Fajr: from dawn until just before sunrise

Zuhr: after midday until afternoon

'Asr: from late afternoon until just before sunset

Maghrib: after sunset until daylight ends

'Isha: night until midnight or dawn

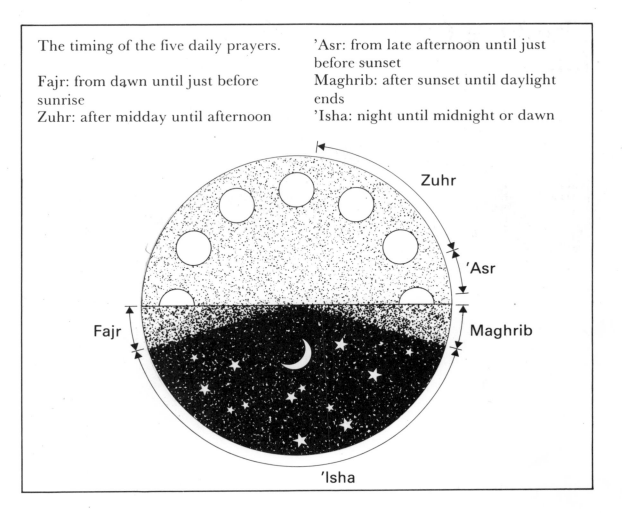

To keep this up may seem hard but if you think about the five prayer times, they do take place at natural breaks in the day: when you get up, around midday (when people in hot countries take a rest from work), at the end of the working day, after supper and before going to sleep.

Performing prayers in the proper way only takes a few minutes. Each period for prayer lasts for about two hours. This means that there is usually plenty of time to slip into a mosque or find somewhere quiet and peaceful at home or work to pray. The one time when everyone is expected to go to the mosque is for midday prayers on Friday, the holy day of Islam.

Before prayer, Muslims wash and take off their shoes. They may unroll a prayer mat to kneel on. Turning in the direction of Makkah, they perform a set of prayer movements with words.

▲ Thousands of pilgrims walking around the Ka'aba in Makkah, Saudi Arabia. To visit the holy city of Makkah and perform certain acts of worship there at least once in their lifetime, is the dream of all Muslims.

Zakat

The Third Pillar of Islam is to give **zakat** once a year. When Muhammad first began preaching the word of God, he told people that they should always treat other people well and help those less fortunate than themselves. By giving some of their savings each year as zakat, Muslims try to make sure that the poor and needy share in the world's wealth. It reminds them that God made the good things in life for everyone, not just for the rich and powerful.

The Fourth Pillar of Islam is to fast during Ramadan. The Fifth and final Pillar is to try to visit the holy city of Makkah at least once in a lifetime.

Pilgrimage

This journey to Makkah is called **'Haj'**. A Muslim who completes the pilgrimage may put the title 'Haji' or 'Hajin' in front of his or her name. The pilgrim performs special acts of worship at the sacred shrine called the **Ka'aba**, and at other holy places around Makkah.

The journey to Makkah from Europe or Africa is much easier today than it was even 100 years ago. Journeys that used to take pilgrims weeks or months and

▲ Every year, about two million Muslims from all parts of the world
make the pilgrimage to Makkah and the holy places which surround it.

which were uncomfortable and sometimes dangerous, can be over in a matter of hours by aeroplane. But travelling to Makkah can still be expensive and exhausting, especially for the many older pilgrims who have spent years saving up for this journey of a lifetime. Yet, however much travelling to Makkah may have changed, its meaning for Muslims is the same as it has always been. However long or hard the journey, the important thing about it is that it brings the pilgrim nearer to God, because it is a journey of the heart and mind, as well as the body. It shows the pilgrim's love of God and it is as important as prayer and belief in God.

When pilgrims arrive in Makkah, they all share the same joy at having reached the holy city. They take part in the same acts of worship and prayer. Women dress simply and men wear the same plain white robes. Everyone looks alike and you can't tell whether someone is rich or poor. Even people's nationalities do not seem to matter. Since everyone has travelled there for the same purpose and with the same feelings, the pilgrims don't need to speak each other's language in order to understand each other.

The importance of sharing

▲ At work, at home or in the mosque, Muslims may use a prayer mat on which to kneel and pray. Some prayer mats are beautifully woven or embroidered.

▲ A wooden prayerboard, which young Muslims use to help them memorise prayers and verses from the Qur'an.

One of the most important feelings a pilgrim has in Makkah is of being part of a 'brotherhood'. All pilgrims know they share the same purpose and beliefs in coming to Makkah, whether they are rich or poor, British or Nigerian, Bangladeshi or Malaysian. This belief in the importance of sharing is, of course, a reason for giving zakat. And the same idea of sharing is repeated in the five daily prayers, because Muslims repeat the same words and movements all over the world. The fact that every Muslim saying prayers turns towards the Ka'aba also adds to this sense of belonging to a worldwide community or brotherhood.

The Qur'an

The Arabic language is something else shared by Muslims, wherever they live. It is the language of worship and prayer, and also of the Qur'an. The Qur'an has been translated into many other languages but most Muslims prefer to read and recite it in Arabic, whatever their own language. As Muslims believe the Qur'an contains the words of God, they feel it is very important not to change these words and their meaning in any way. A copy of the Qur'an printed today is the same, word for word, as the very first handwritten copy.

Arabic is a very old and poetic language. Some words have several meanings. It can be difficult to express these same meanings in just one word of another language. Translations can therefore change the sense and feeling of the original words. Arabic is also a very musical language. When the Qur'an is recited or read, it sounds very beautiful. When it is read aloud in other languages, the musical sound to the words is often lost. So Muslim children start learning Arabic and memorising parts of the Qur'an when they are very young.

Action

Action, or practising what you believe, is as important to Muslims as belief itself. Being a Muslim affects how you behave in every bit of your life, not just during prayer and worship. So the Qur'an is really a guide to all parts of a Muslim's life. It contains advice on how to behave to their friends and family and the people they work with, what they should and should not eat, how to run a business, how to deal with marriage and death, and many other things. It contains advice for Islamic governments too. For example, it tells them how to deal with matters of law and education. So the Qur'an not only guides Muslims in their relationship with God, but in their relationships with each other.

Ramadan — the month of fasting

Senegalese children with their ▶ prayerboards. Young children are not expected to fast during Ramadan. Once they are about ten years old, however, they may try to fast for the whole month.

Muslims give Zakat ul-Fitr before ▶▶ taking part in the Eid prayers at the end of Ramadan. The money is used to make sure that everyone, rich and poor, can share in the food and festivities of Eid.

◀ A Bangladeshi rolls out a mat before saying his prayers. Muslims not only fast during Ramadan. It is a time when they try to think especially hard about God and the importance of following the teachings of the Qur'an.

So now you know how important the ideas of sharing and of being part of a brotherhood are in Islam. One of the things which helps people fast during Ramadan is knowing that, all over the world, other Muslims are sharing the same pangs of hunger and the same determination to succeed. And by giving some extra zakat at Eid, called **Zakat ul-Fitr**, Muslims remember those who are less well-off than themselves and help them share in the joy of the festival too. Zakat ul-Fitr should be equal to the cost of one meal for every member of the family.

Anyone who is ill, very old or expecting a baby is not expected to fast. Nor are young children, who may try just one or two days' fasting. But once they are about ten, all Muslims who can fast try to keep it up for the whole month. Of course, there will be times when someone could have a small snack and nobody would know. This makes fasting a very special way for a Muslim to show God his or her love, because only they and God really know whether they are succeeding.

Fasting from sunrise to sunset may seem a difficult thing to do but Ramadan is not a gloomy time at all. Everyone keeps each other's spirits up. Friends meet and chat together, but no food or drink is served at home or in restaurants until sunset. When Ramadan comes during the hottest part of the summer, shops and offices in some Muslim countries in the Middle East may close down during the day. As the sky darkens, everything comes to life again. The lights come on in cafes and restaurants. Cinemas, shops, bazaars and even some offices fill up with people again. Families get together to share the evening meal, called **iftar**. It is a happy time when everyone feels the satisfaction of having completed another day of fasting.

Families living in non-Muslim countries may miss the special atmosphere and activities which take place during the month of Ramadan. They may make up for this by inviting friends around to share iftar or by joining others in their local mosque for special Ramadan prayers.

The meaning of Ramadan

▲Young Muslim girls singing a religious song at Eid celebrations.

It can also be hard for someone keeping Ramadan in a non-Muslim country as they might find themselves one of only a few people at school or work going without food and drink all day. But they have the satisfaction of knowing they are doing something very important for God. For Ramadan means much more to Muslims than giving up food and drink. The experience of fasting teaches Muslims many things.

It gives them an idea of what it really is like to be poor and have an empty stomach. This reminds people of their own good fortune and of how important it is to remember others who are less fortunate by giving zakat. It also helps people to learn how not to give into selfish, lazy or greedy feelings. People encourage each other when they feel weak-willed and, like anything for which we must make an extra effort, the satisfaction Muslims feel when they succeed in completing Ramadan is very special.

The Muslim calendar is based on the 12 cycles of the moon in a year. It has roughly 11 days less than the Western solar calendar. This means that the dates of Ramadan and Eid ul-Fitr gradually move through all the seasons, since they start about 11 days earlier each year.

1983
RAMADAN   SHAWWAL

● ◐ ◑ ◯ ◯ ◯ ◑ ◐   EID
1 2 3 4 5 6 7 8 9 10 11 12 13 14 15 16 17 18 19 20 21 22 23 24 25 26 27 28 29 30 1 2 3

JUNE   JULY
11 12 13 14 15 16 17 18 19 20 21 22 23 24 25 26 27 28 29 30 1 2 3 4 5 6 7 8 9 10 11 12 13

1984
RAMADAN   SHAWWAL

● ◐ ◑ ◯ ◯ ◯ ◑ ◐ ●
1 2 3 4 5 6 7 8 9 10 11 12 13 14 15 16 17 18 19 20 21 22 23 24 25 26 27 28 29 30 EID
                                                                                  1 2 3

MAY JUNE   JULY
31 1 2 3 4 5 6 7 8 9 10 11 12 13 14 15 16 17 18 19 20 21 22 23 24 25 26 27 28 29 30 1 2

Ramadan is also a time when Muslims make an extra effort to be kind to other people. They avoid mean or angry words and behaviour. They should not tell lies or break promises. Above all, it is a time to think especially hard about God. Those who can, spend a lot of time praying and studying at the mosque. Some Muslims will read part of the Qur'an every day so as to complete it by the end of the month. Each night there are extra prayers at the mosque which many people try to attend. These are called **Taraweeh salat**.

The Night of Power

The night on which the Angel Gabriel first visited Muhammad in the cave on Mount Hira took place in the last ten days of the month. This important occasion is known as the Night of Power. Most people think that it took place on the 27th day of Ramadan, although the exact date is not known. Many Muslims spend these last ten days in their mosque, concentrating all their thoughts and prayers on God. Some mosques may provide food and space to sleep for a hundred or more Muslims at this time. This last period of Ramadan ends in the way we described in the first pages of this book, with the sighting of the new moon. Once the silver arc of the moon has risen and been seen in the sky, the month of fasting officially ends and the happy feast of Eid ul-Fitr begins.

Eid ul-Fitr

▶ Young British Muslims gather together in their new clothes for Eid celebrations.

There are Muslims living all over the world. This map shows the countries where there are large numbers of Muslims. ▶

◀ In northern Nigeria, Muslims celebrate Eid at special fairs called Sallah. Everyone dresses up in beautiful robes and parades in front of the Emir's palace on foot, on camels and on horseback.

Eid ul-Fitr begins with an early morning meal. Then everyone gathers together for special Eid prayers. As so many people take part, the service may be held outside the mosque in a large area big enough to take hundreds, perhaps thousands, of worshippers.

Usually the **imam** (prayer leader) gives a short talk first. He reminds people of the purpose and meaning of Ramadan. The prayers which follow can be an awe-inspiring sight, as thousands of people together follow the movements and recite the words of the prayer leader. There is always a great sense of joy and excitement. After prayers people walk around hugging and greeting each other. Some exchange gifts of flowers and sweets. Everyone wears their best clothes, usually newly bought for Eid.

The Muslim world

Although Arabic history and language are such important parts of the story of Islam, most Muslims are not Arabs. The

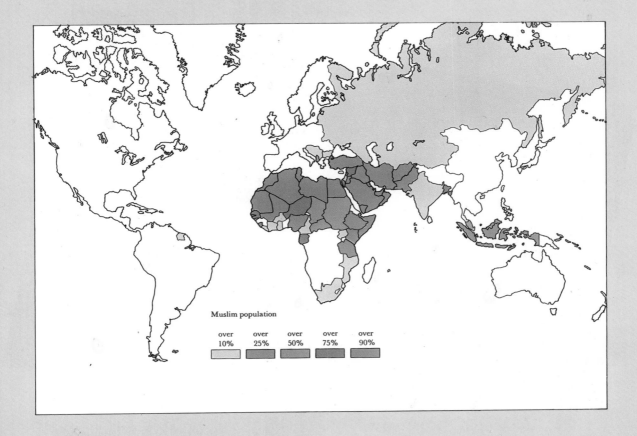

Muslim population

| over 10% | over 25% | over 50% | over 75% | over 90% |

countries with the largest numbers of Muslims are Indonesia, Bangladesh, India and Pakistan. There are many millions of Muslims in Africa, particularly in West Africa. More Europeans follow Islam than any other religion apart from Christianity. Muslims share many traditions and ways of doing things as well as their beliefs, perhaps more than followers of other world religions. Yet, as you might expect, with so many millions of Muslims living in different countries, cultures and climates, the Muslim world contains many different patterns of living.

In the same way that mosques all over the world look different but express the same ideas about God, so different groups of Muslims have developed their own special customs, including Eid celebrations. So Muslims in Nigeria, Bangladesh and Saudi Arabia will wear different styles of dress for Eid, eat different foods and celebrate in their own way, but their feelings of joy and thanks to God are the same as those felt by Muslims all over the world.

▲ A Malaysian family enjoying delicious cakes and sweets at Eid. Most of the festival's celebrations take place at home with close friends and family.

Eid celebrations

As you might expect, one of the pleasures of Eid ul-Fitr everywhere is sharing good food with friends and family. People visit each other's homes, often bringing gifts of sweets, dried fruits and sugared almonds. Children may be offered small presents of money, nuts and sweets. Houses are decorated with colourful Eid cards. The covers of the cards may show a beautiful mosque, or be decorated with some writing or Islamic designs and patterns. Inside there are greetings such as 'Eid Mubarak', which means 'Happy Festival'.

As well as their new clothes, girls and women may wear some delicate and pretty patterns on their hands. They paint these on with henna. This is a brown dye made from the leaves of a plant. Both men and women may put on some of the sweet scent called **itar** before going to the Eid prayers. Sometimes there will be a fair or entertainers in town during Eid.

▼ Eid celebrations in northern Nigeria.

Eid in Nigeria

In northern Nigeria, where there are about 50 million Muslims, the celebrations at the end of Ramadan are some of the most colourful and exciting in the world. In large towns such as Katsina and Kano, the Emir (who is the local ruler) leads the morning prayers outside in the main prayer-ground.

Afterwards, everyone gathers in front of the Emir's palace to watch or take part in wonderful parades.

Some people are on foot and others are on horseback. Some ride tall, swaying camels. Everyone is dressed in beautiful, brightly coloured robes and costumes. The air is full of the sound of musical instruments and drums. In the crowd, jugglers and other entertainers add to the fun and excitement. The horses and camels themselves are decorated with silver bridles, embroidered saddle cloths and multi-coloured tassles. These Eid celebrations are called **Sallah**.

Eid in Britain

Eid celebrations in a non-Muslim northern country such as Britain may not be as colourful as they are in Nigeria but it is an equally happy time. At this mosque in Southall, west London, over 2500 people come to the morning prayers. In fact, there are so many people that they have to have three sets of Eid prayers. And each time the prayer hall and the car park in front of the mosque are completely full.

All the side streets around the mosque are crowded with people in their best clothes greeting their friends and families. Many of these families have parents or grandparents who have come to live in England from Pakistan or Bangladesh. A lot of the girls and women dress in beautiful loose trousers and tunics, called shalwar kameez, or in saris. Many of the boys wear white clothes with an embroidered waistcoat and a small white cap.

The imam stands at the entrance of the mosque and greets people as they come in. Also at the door are people collecting last-minute Zakat ul-Fitr offerings. The

▲ Friends and relatives greet each other outside the mosque after Eid congregational prayers in Southall.

◀ So many people come to the Eid prayers at this mosque in Southall, London, that they fill the car park in front of the prayer hall.

▼ Imams usually run classes in the early evening or at weekends so that British Muslim children can learn all about the Qur'an and its teachings.

mosque committee usually gathers well over £4000, which they give to many local charities and organisations to help others. Families in the area all take care to see that their own relatives, especially the older ones, are well looked after at Eid. Those with sons or daughters scattered in other parts of the country try to get everyone back together for the festival. For days before the end of Ramadan, shops in Southall and other parts of London, Bradford, Birmingham, Liverpool, Cardiff and Sheffield where there are large Muslim communities, sell Eid cards and sweets.

There are more than one million Muslims and over 300 mosques in Britain. On the morning of Eid ul-Fitr, these mosques all over the country are as full as the one in Southall. For the next three days families and friends meet and celebrate in their own homes. Some people take these days off work, for Eid is not a holiday in Britain as it would be a Muslim country. Above all, British Muslims, like Muslims all over the world, enjoy being with their families in this festival, which centres around happy meals and celebrations in the home.

A world of difference

▶ Children taking part in some Eid celebrations in Britain. In 1983 Ramadan was in June and July. It came at a time of school exams for some British Muslim children. Each year, Ramadan starts about 11 days earlier. In 1990 it will be in March.

Eid celebrations are not the only things about Ramadan which may differ around the world. Going through the day without food or drink in the very hot climate of Saudi Arabia, for example, can be much harder than it is in the cooler weather of northern Europe. But there are many more hours of daylight in an English or Swedish summer, for example, than in countries nearer the Equator, so fasting can last much longer.

Hours of daylight

The Qur'an says fasting should begin as soon as there is enough light from the rising sun to tell a white thread from a black one. So, to get through the day, most Muslims have a meal very early in the morning before dawn breaks. Their fast must then continue until the sun sets. In countries near the Equator this is usually about 12 hours later. Daylight generally lasts from about 6 am to 6 pm, winter and summer. During a British summer, however, fasting may have to start as early as 3 am and go on until 9 pm or even later.

However, there are fewer than twelve hours of daylight in some winter months in northern Europe. So when the month of Ramadan coincides with, say December or January, a Muslim in Europe would fast for a shorter time than his 'brothers' in the Middle East. And Ramadan does come at a slightly different time each year — about 11 days earlier each time, in fact.

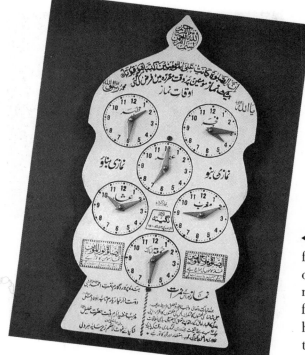

◀ This board shows the times for the five daily prayers in a British mosque one May. Prayer times are based on the movement of the sun. In countries far from the Equator, such as Britain, the hours of prayer may change a lot through the seasons.

The Muslim calendar

The twelve months of the Muslim calendar are based on the waxing and waning of the moon. It has 354 days. The solar calendar used in the West is based on the movement of the sun around the earth, which takes 365 days. The Muslim lunar calendar does not add any 'leap' days to make up for the 11 days less it has than the solar calendar. So each year any date in the Muslim calendar usually takes place 11 days earlier than it did the year before. It takes about 33 years for the month of Ramadan to go right through the seasons.

Hours of prayer

The greater contrasts between the weather and the hours of daylight during the seasons in countries far from the Equator affects Muslim worship in other ways too. For example, the times of the five daily prayers take place at natural breaks in the day. These are based on the movement of the sun in the sky, from dawn to dusk. They were established in Arabia, where there is little change between summer and winter. But a Muslim in northern Europe would find the hours of winter prayers very different from those of summer. There can be as much as five hours' difference between summer and winter sunsets, for example.

A world of change

◄ A medical clinic, Brunei. Better standards of education have helped some Muslim women take up skilled jobs, although after marriage they are expected to put the family first.

About one person out of every six people in the world is Muslim. Different surroundings, national and local customs affect the way they live all over the world. So do modern developments and changes in world affairs. From time to time, religious scholars discuss whether these might affect Islamic customs and traditions in any part of the worldwide Islamic community. Whenever there are questions about Islamic practices and traditions, scholars and statesmen look to the Qur'an for advice and guidance. They base their answers on its teachings.

International events may bring leaders of Muslim countries together to take important decisions. The great wealth that oil has brought many Arab countries has enabled them to work together to help many poorer Muslim countries.

However different their patterns of living, Muslims are always guided by the words of the Qur'an. It teaches that Islam is a religion which reaches the hearts of people wherever and whenever they live. Women in one country, such as Iran, may wear traditional Islamic dress; women of other nationalities may often wear western clothes. Better standards of education in many countries have enabled some women to take up skilled jobs. Others may stay within the family home most of

◄ Science graduates at Dhaka university, Bangladesh. The wealth which oil has brought some Arab countries has enabled them to help poorer Muslim countries, such as Bangladesh, with their development.

▶ Strong and happy family relationships are a very important part of the Muslim way of life. This Moroccan boy will have been brought up to show love and respect to older relatives such as his grandfather. In turn, he will expect his own children to care for him in his old age.

their lives. A stable and happy family life, which includes grandparents, aunts, uncles and cousins, is at the heart of the Muslim way of life.

Some Muslim countries keep to purely Islamic ways of running themselves and have no laws or forms of entertainment, for example, which do not meet the ideals or beliefs expressed in the Qur'an. Other countries with large numbers of Muslims have adopted some Western practices and ideas, without changing their basic beliefs or customs.

Unchanging faith

In Europe, North America and the West Indies, many Muslims have become important members of the local, non-Muslim community without losing any of their Islamic character or customs. They set up and run their own mosques, clubs, charities and religion schools, so that their children can grow up knowing what it means to be a follower of Islam.

They will learn that when they say their prayers they are not alone but part of a worldwide community of millions who, five times every day, turn in the direction of the same holy shrine and perform the same act of worship, unchanged for over a thousand years.

Acknowledgements

The author and publishers would like to thank
Urvashi Butalia and Richard Tames for their help
in the preparation of the book.

The author and publishers wish to acknowledge
the following photographic sources:
Amena Pictures, pages 6, 7, 14, 15, 19, 31
The British Library, pages 9,17
Middle East Photographic Archive, page 4
P.W. Syme, page 22
Liba Taylor, pages 19, 26, 27, 29

The remaining photographs used in this book
were provided by the Commonwealth Institute.

Designed by
The Tandem Design Company, Reading.

First published 1986

Published by
MACMILLAN EDUCATION LTD
Houndmills, Basingstoke, Hampshire RG21 2XS
and London
Companies and representatives
throughout the world

ISBN 0 333 37898 9

Printed in Hong Kong